The Dog That Gave My Brother Words

By Wendy Hinote Lanier 🐾 Illustrated by Jieting Chen

To Boyd and the puppies for always making life sweeter.

End Game Press books may be purchased in bulk at special discounts for sales promotion, corporate gifts, ministry, fund-raising, or educational purposes. Special editions can also be created to specifications. For details, contact Special Sales Dept., End Game Press, P.O. Box 206, Nesbit, MS 38651 or info@endgamepress.com. Visit our website at www.endgamepress.com.

ISBN: 978-1-63797-060-7 | eBook ISBN: 978-1-63797-061-4 | Library of Congress Control Number: 2022939880

Published in association with Cyle Young of the Cyle Young Literary Elite, LLC.

Cover & Interior Design by Tamara Dever, TLC Book Design, TLCBookDesign.com | Illustrated by Jieting Chen, the Bright Agency

Printed in China

10 9 8 7 6 5 4 3 2 1

We're getting a dog! A dog for Sam.

Sam is my little brother.
He loves wearing hats,
watching videos on
his tablet, and his
bean bag cocoon.

He is also autistic.

Autistic is a word that describes someone who sees and feels things differently. For Sam, it's as though he lives in his own little world.

Most of the time, I am not invited.

But sometimes Sam
lets me help him build
things with Legos, or we
play a game on his tablet.
And he likes it when
I read to him—especially
books about the ocean.
Sometimes, if he really
likes the story, his large
brown eyes actually look
into mine, and he smiles.
But only sometimes.
And he never speaks.

Most of the time, Sam sits alone—in his cocoon playing
on his tablet or spinning his fidget toy really fast. My mom
says Sam is smart, but I m not sure how she knows that.

When Sam is at home and everything is calm and familiar,
he is quiet and looks like any other eight-year-old boy.

But, sometimes, if we go to a restaurant where it's noisy or if the mall gets too crowded, he screams and flaps his hands until we take him home. Mom says sometimes going out and doing things that aren't part of Sam's normal routine can be too much for him. She calls it sensory overload. I call it embarrassing.

A couple of years ago, there was an autistic
kid in my class. He had a therapy dog to
help him with school and people and stuff.
The dog helped keep him calm, and all
the other kids thought it was really cool.
My parents and I talked about it and
decided Sam should have one, too.
We think maybe, if Sam has a therapy dog,
he will be able to talk and laugh and
go places like other boys his age.

The only problem is therapy dogs are really expensive. For over a year now, we've been saving to buy one. We skipped our vacation, held bake sales and fundraisers, and my dad even applied for a grant. That's like a loan you don't have to pay back. With all of it together, we finally have enough. We found an organization that trains and places therapy dogs, and they helped us find the perfect one.

And now, today is the day!
Today, my brother is going to
meet a dog
named Lexi.

We're all excited…and a little worried.
What if Sam doesn't like the dog?
What if he freaks out?
My mom is mostly worried.
My dad says we have to try.
I'm not sure what to think.

My brother is in the den, sitting in his cocoon,
when the doorbell rings. I hear muffled voices
as my parents answer the door. I feel like I should
be near Sam—just in case. So, I sit cross-legged
on the floor next to his chair.

Then a lady enters the room with a chocolate-colored Labrador Retriever on a leash. She stands across the room from Sam.

In a soft voice, she says,
"Sam, this is Lexi."

My brother does not appear to notice at first.
But slowly he turns to look at the dog.
Lexi begins moving toward him. She never
takes her eyes off Sam's face. When she finally
reaches him, Lexi puts her head on Sam's knee.

Sam shoots me a quick look, and his eyes
are sparkling. I have never seen them
do that before.

"You can pet Lexi if you like," the lady says. "Like this."

My brother watches her. Then slowly he reaches out his hand
to rest it on Lexi's head.

My mother begins to cry. My dad puts
his arm around her. He looks
a little teary-eyed, too.

Lexi nuzzles my brother's hand, and he laughs.
"Sarah, look!"

It is the first time I have ever heard my brother
say my name. I didn't know he could.

Lexi roots her nose under Sam's arm, inviting him
to put his arms around her. My brother slides
off his chair and joins her on the floor.
Within minutes, he is sprawled next to her,
stroking her fur.

"Good dog," Sam says. "Good Lexi."

My mom, dad, and I can hardly believe it. Six words.
Six whole words. It's only six, but to us, each word
is like a miracle. It gives us hope there will be
more. We know there are no guarantees,
but that's okay. For today, it is enough.

Today a dog named Lexi
gave my brother words.

AUTISM IS A DEVELOPMENTAL DISORDER THAN CAN AFFECT THE WAY A PERSON interacts with others, communicates, or behaves. Children with autism often have very focused interests and/or may engage in repetitive behaviors. In 2013, all autism disorders became identified as ASD (autism spectrum disorder). Asperger syndrome, for example, is a type of autism.

Not everyone with autism exhibits the same abilities and/or disabilities. Only about one-third of people on the autism spectrum are nonverbal. Some children with autism have above average intelligence, while others may have learning disabilities or below average intelligence. There is no one type of autism.

People who work with autistic children have reported mixed results when introducing therapy dogs. However, having one can sometimes make a world of difference. Therapy dogs allow some children with autism to successfully navigate social situations and lead more normal lives with much less stress.

KIDS WANT TO KNOW:

CAN YOU CATCH AUTISM? Autism is about how a person sees and experiences the world around them. You can't catch it. But you CAN learn to be patient with someone who has it. You can treat autistic people kindly and never allow anyone else to be mean to them. Most autistic people enjoy having friends and participating in many of the same activities as you. Just be kind and patient. Who knows? That autistic kid on your baseball team could turn out to be your best friend.

WHAT IS A MELTDOWN? Autistic people are often very sensitive to light, sound, taste, and/or touch. They tend to experience these things more intensely than most people. This can cause discomfort or even pain. When the discomfort or pain gets to be too much, the person may scream, cry, lash out at others, or try to hurt themselves. It causes a big scene, but an autistic person who has reached this "sensory overload" loses the ability to control themselves. You can help by being calm, quiet, and stopping whatever activity seems to be causing the overload.

WHAT ARE FIDGET TOYS? Fidget toys give autistic kids something to do with their hands. This helps them control their need for movement and touch. Such toys can help them remain calm, focused, and attentive.

HOW CAN YOU HELP SOMEONE GET A THERAPY DOG? Trained therapy and other assistance dogs can cost more than $35,000. Organizations such as Paws with a Cause train and provide dogs for those that need them. You can help these organizations by donating money, volunteering, raising a puppy, or providing a home for a parent dog.

WHY A LABRADOR RETRIEVER? Any kind of dog can be a therapy dog. But Labrador Retrievers and Golden Retrievers (or a mix of the two) are the most common for kids with autism. These breeds are calm, easy to train, and have a great temperament. They are also large enough to serve as a kind of weighted blanket to help calm a child with autism.

CAN YOU PLAY WITH A THERAPY DOG? You should NEVER attempt to pet or play with a service animal of any kind without the permission of the owner. And when the animal is working is not a good time to ask. It's very tempting, but distracting a service animal could cause harm or injury to the person they are supposed to be helping. It is best to admire service animals from a distance unless the owner gives you permission.

To find out more, visit AutismSociety.org.
To find out more about therapy dogs for people with autism and other disabilities, visit PawsWithACause.org.